It's the First Day of Kindergarten, CHLoe Zoe!

Jane Smith

Albert Whitman & Company
Chicago, Illinois

It's the first day of kindergarten!

Kindergarten is a place to discover and learn exciting things with a teacher and a class full of new and old friends.

Mommy and Daddy told me in kindergarten I will get to learn my ABCs and 123s, sing and play, and read and write.

Last year, preschool was so much fun! That's where I met my friends Mary Margaret and George. I already know I love school.

This year I have a new, bigger backpack with a matching lunch box. I'm all ready!

When we arrive at my new school, it is bigger and busier than I expected. There are so many kids—big and little—getting dropped off. My belly does a nervous somersault.

"I wish I was old enough to go to school like you," says my little sister, Sophie.

"You will be old enough soon," I say. I smile at her bravely.

I say good-bye to my family once
I see my friends Mary Margaret and
George standing outside the two
kindergarten classrooms.

One classroom is called the sunshine room and the other is
the rainbow room. I wave hello to my friends. Mary Margaret
waves back, but she looks really upset!

"What's wrong, Mary Margaret?" I ask.

"George and I are in the rainbow room class. But *your* class is in the sunshine room." She frowns.

"We're not all in the same class!" George groans.

"Oh, no!" I say. Suddenly I feel queasy. Mary Margaret starts to cry.

I start to cry too.

"Don't worry, Chloe Zoe," George says.

"We'll see you at recess for sure."

It is hard saying good-bye to my friends.

I walk into the sunshine room alone.
I hope George is right.

My new teacher, Teacher Emily, rounds up everyone for circle time. We start with the "Good Morning" song. Then we learn each other's names.

Next, Teacher Emily asks for a helper. Another girl, Jessie, raises her hand. She gets to share the date: Wednesday, September 2. Jessie seems a little nervous, so I smile at her.

SEPTEMBER

SU	M	TU	W	TH	F	S
		1	2	3		
6	7	8	9	10		
13	14	15	16	17		
20	21	22				
27	28	29	3			

The whole class sings the ABC song together. I wish my friends were singing with me.

George always forgets the letter K and Mary Margaret always sings the loudest. I miss them.

During snack time, I see Violet sitting all by herself. Violet
and her twin sister, Vivian, were in my preschool class last year.
Vivian must be in the rainbow room. I join Violet and she smiles.

At center time, Jessie asks if she can sit with Violet and me. "Of course!" I say. Ben and Billy join us. I am surrounded by old and new friends!

We practice counting shapes and writing numbers. One triangle, two circles, three squares, four hearts, and five stars.

The sunshine room has easels for us to use. For our first art project, everyone paints an apple. Mine is red with a friendly worm. I am having so much fun I forget Mary Margaret and George aren't with me!

Then the whole class lines up for recess. I keep a close lookout for my friends. I hope they have been having fun in their classroom.

I wave to George and Mary Margaret.
They run across the playground to
join me.

Mary Margaret and George have Vivian, Leo, and their new friend, Lily, with them. "Kindergarten is SO much fun!" Mary Margaret gushes.

"SO much fun!" I agree. "Come on! Let's play tag!" Everyone laughs and we all run off.

At the end of the day, everyone's families come to pick them up from their classrooms. I meet George and Mary Margaret in the hallway.

"I really missed you guys today!" I tell them.

"We missed you too!" Mary Margaret says. "But somehow kindergarten was even more fun than preschool!"

"Awesome!" says George. "This is going to be the best school year ever!"

"Happy first day of kindergarten, everyone!" I cheer.

For more Chloe Zoe fun
—like crafts, coloring pages, games, and activities—
visit www.albertwhitman.com.

For my kindergarten superstar, Phoebe Love

Also available:
It's Valentine's Day, Chloe Zoe! • It's Easter, Chloe Zoe!
It's the First Day of Preschool, Chloe Zoe!

More Chloe Zoe books coming soon:
It's Halloween, Chloe Zoe!
It's Thanksgiving, Chloe Zoe!

Library of Congress Cataloging-in-Publication data is on file with the publisher.

Text and pictures copyright © 2016 by Jane Smith
Published in 2016 by Albert Whitman & Company
ISBN 978-0-8075-2458-9

Printed in China
10 9 8 7 6 5 4 3 2 1 HH 24 23 22 21 20 19 18 17 16

Design by Jordan Kost

For more information about Albert Whitman & Company, visit our web site at www.albertwhitman.com.